For all the great little kids learning to respect themselves and to respect others!

For Florence, my sister, my friend who is always there for me.
— L.G.

For Sean, the one who was there when I needed a friend the most, a kindred spirit from the bottom of the high school food chain.
— P.B.

NATIONAL LIBRARY OF CANADA CATALOGUING IN PUBLICATION DATA

Grossman, Linda Sky
Respect is correct

(I'm a great little kid series)
Published in conjunction with Toronto Child Abuse Centre
ISBN 1-896764-58-4 (bound).—ISBN 1-896764-56-8 (pbk.)

1. Self-esteem—Juvenile fiction. I. Bockus, Petra II. Toronto Child Abuse Centre
III. Title. IV. Series: Grossman, Linda Sky I'm a great little kid series.

PS8563.R65R48 2002   jC813'.6   C2001-904301-5
PZ7.G9084Re 2002

Printed in Hong Kong, China

Toronto Child Abuse Centre gratefully acknowledges the support of the Ontario Trillium Foundation, which provided funding for the I'm A Great Little Kid project. Further funding was generously provided by TD Securities.

Second Story Press gratefully acknowledges the assistance of the Ontario Arts Council and the Canada Council for the Arts for our publishing program. We acknowledge the financial support of the Government of Canada through the Book Publishing Industry Development Program.

ONTARIO ARTS COUNCIL
CONSEIL DES ARTS DE L'ONTARIO

Published by
SECOND STORY PRESS
720 Bathurst Street, Suite 301
Toronto, ON
M5S 2R4

www.secondstorypress.on.ca

Respect Is Correct

By Linda Sky Grossman

Illustrated by Petra Bockus

Second Story Press

Amon, are you listening, I'm talking to you,
I'm not going back, I've had it, I'm through!
I'm tired of the teacher and her golden rule,
I don't like the things we're learning in school.

I'm telling you, Amon, it doesn't seem fair,

I'm sick of being teased about my frizzy red hair.

I'm short and I'm never on the best team,

I try to smile, but I'd like to scream!

Because I wear glasses, they make fun of me.

They don't understand, glasses help me to see!

I hate it when they call me freckle-face,

I wish I could send them to outer space!

But this new project really takes the cake,

I'd like to tell the teacher to jump in a lake.

We're supposed to explain what respect means.

I'm going to tear my paper into smithereens!

"Create a picture or a skit that shows respect."

It means nothing to me; it's a dumb subject!

So now do you see why I don't want to go?

I have no picture, no skit, nothing to show.

I know what you mean, Jennie, and I understand.

When they tease me, I want to stick my head in the sand!

They tell me I have a dirty face,

And my slanted eyes are out of place.

Sometimes I think I'd like to say,

I don't see why we can't *all* play.

It's mean to pick on one another,

Because under our skin, we're the same as each other.

Jennie, look at that lady over there,

The one the kids are trying to scare.

Her dog's leash is tangled by her side,

She looks as if she has no place to hide!

Come on, Jennie, let's get out of here,

Those kids are bullies, don't go near!

Jennie, hurry, let's run away,

You'll get hurt if you go, I'd rather play!

We'll get some help, Amon, don't be afraid,

I know those kids, they're in a higher grade.

There's a teacher, go get him now!

Maybe he can stop this somehow.

The teacher came running on the double,

He could see the lady was really in trouble!

"I don't call this the right way to play!

Leave her alone, do you hear what I say?"

Jennie asked, "Excuse me, are you okay?

We know those kids who have all run away.

Here, let us help, we'll lend a hand,

Steady now, do you think you can stand?

Amon and I are sorry you have had such a fright,

We are going into school now, if you're all right.

We have to talk about respect today,

And I have no idea what to say!"

Later in class, the teacher called out, "No noise!

Let's discuss your project now, girls and boys.

Respect is something we can give away,

But first we must earn it every day."

"This morning the principal had an unusual call,
It seems that a lady was caught in a brawl.
She asked if I know a bubbly, red-haired child,
One who is polite, and not the least bit wild.

The lady said there was a boy who helped, too,
I think I know who it was, don't you?
Jennie and Amon, have you something to say,
About what happened near the school today?"

"The lady said she had great pride
In those two kids who came to her side.
She said they showed a level of respect
That was far greater than she would expect.

Children, I can tell by what you did today,
That you understand respect in every way!
Your real-life skit was absolutely first-rate,
I hope that you both feel really great!"

Respect is not a thing we can touch,

Although we all need it, oh so much!

Jennie felt special and ten feet tall.

School wasn't so bad after all!

For Grown-ups

About Respect

Respecting others is about treating people the way we want to be treated. It means paying attention to feelings, ideas, bodies, property and the desire for privacy. We show respect through our actions, our words and our appreciation of individuality. Teaching children about their rights and the rights of others demonstrates the importance of respect. Everyone deserves to be treated with respect.

Parents can support their children to learn the importance of respect:

Show respect: listen to what others have to say.

Talk openly: all feelings and ideas are valuable and important and can be talked about.

Set an example: treat everyone in the family fairly, providing opportunities for all family members that respect their interests and abilities.

Respect everyone's privacy: recognize that children have a right to privacy, and respect age-appropriate boundaries when it comes to their personal space, bodies and possessions.

Appreciate people's differences: participate in events and activities that give children the opportunity to share in and appreciate the beliefs and customs of others.

For more information: **www.tcac.on.ca**